PUERTO RiCO

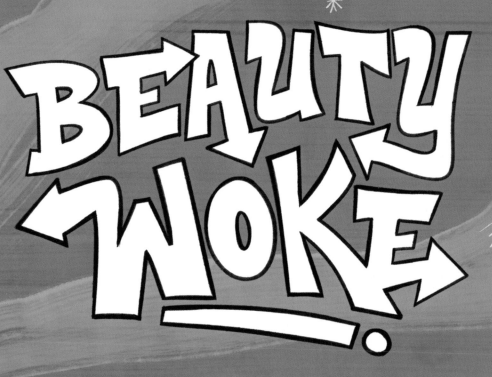

BEAUTY WOKE

Written by NoNieqa Ramos

Illustrated by Paola Escobar

VERSIFY

Houghton Mifflin Harcourt

Boston   New York

Beauty sleeps.

In the dark
is where it starts.
First there is one heart,
then two.
One day,
something new:
little conch shell ears to hear;
watercolor words drawing near
like estas palabras—

SUEÑO HECHO REALIDAD

LOVE

HOPE

FELICIDAD

But from la doctora, words of alarm:
"Not even Baby's safe from harm.
Keep Beauty close.
The world ain't woke."

She said, "They got spells.
Words that devour.
They'll sentence her to sleep
and take her power."

So, los padres safety-proofed;
had la espiritista bless every room.

Finally,
water breaks.
Beauty wakes!

Light.
Arms.
Warmth.
Space.
Mamá's face!

¡Bienvenida!
¡Qué linda!
She already turned her head!
She. Is. PERFECT.

Beauty woke. Beauty slept.
La familia checked Beauty's every breath.

Un día, Beauty spoke
palabras like song notes:

¡MAMÁ!

¡PAPÁ!

¡ABUELA!

¡TÍA!

¡MADRINA!

¡FAMILIA!

BEAUTY!

Then:
Beauty's first parade.
Relatives showed up
from Pelham Bay
and White Plains.

Wrapped in her flag, Beauty slept,
crowned by the crowd
BABY BORINQUEN.

Soon, she outgrew shoe after shoe.
Time for Beauty to get schooled.

Abuela came out the kitchen;
said, "Stand up, nena. Listen.
Did you know
your blood runs onyx, gold?"
Beauty shook her head.
"Now you been told."

"Lay your hand on your head.
Say Taíno Indian.
Say African.
Lay your hand on your heart.
Say Boricua."

Abuela said,
"Beauty, change. Beauty, grow.
But stay onyx. Stay gold."

Beauty said, "Sí, lo haré. Yes, I WILL."

She felt as strong as the bull.
Like the hummingbird:
BEAUTY—FUL.

Until un día,
Beauty had nothin' better to do.
Sat with Tío to watch the news.

Saw people that looked like family,
but heard words that hurt,
like

DANGEROUS

DIRTY

LAZY

She thought,
ARE THEY TALKING ABOUT ME?

Her blood wasn't running onyx, gold.
It was running cold.
Beauty's mood: confused.
Her heart bruisin'
black and blue.
Beauty had to know the truth.

She laced up her sneaks.
Threw her hair in a bun.

While her familia prepped for the parade,
Beauty went on the run.

But no matter where she turned,
the palabras cut, burned:

Beauty ran home.
Drew the shades.
Her heart ached.
She fell asleep.
Didn't dream.

El próximo día was the parade.
But Beauty threw shade.
Wear the durags
of Puerto Rican flags
her tías sewed?
YEAH, NO.

Wear her hoops of gold?
WHAT FOR?

Dance bomba and plena?
¡QUÉ VERGÜENZA!

La familia knew right then:
Beauty's eyes were open,
but she was sleepwalkin'.

"911!" Mami yelled. "¡Emergencia!
Time to call in the whole familia!"

In a circle, la familia stood
with a bunch of vecinos from the 'hood.
And la bisabuela needed no introduction—
she was running this production.

In español and inglés, this is what la bisabuela said:
"**¡Escuchen!** Listen to me. Ain't nobody gonna school us on beauty."

"WORD!" La familia nodded their heads.

"Spanish is magic," la bisabuela said.

"WORD!" la familia said. "AMEN!"

"Black is **beauty-ful.**
Black is a power.
Say it."
They said it.
"Say it again."
They said it louder.

Abuela said,
"Let us lay our hands on Beauty.
Bestow on her our blessings.
Nena, you are a gift.
You are EVERYTHING.
Cumple tu destino.
Fulfill your destiny."

After the laying on of hands,
Beauty said, "I think I understand."
With each whisper,
each palabra sagrada,
grew a seed.
Beauty opened her eyes wide.
Thought,
I CAN FINALLY SEE:

Under the ancestors' watchful eyes,
the eternal circle
of her tribe,
linked with strength,
not with chains,
the blood of Borinquen
running through her veins.

Lit with resistance,
imagination,
hope.
Rooted in truth,

Beauty was **WOKE.**

To my beauties, Jandilee and Langston Everlee:
Wokeness is a journey, not a destination.
—N.R.

To my grandmothers, Clara and Floralba, with love
—P.E.

Text copyright © 2022 by NoNieqa Ramos
Illustrations copyright © 2022 by Paola Escobar

Versify® is an imprint of Houghton Mifflin Harcourt Publishing Company.
Versify is a registered trademark of Houghton Mifflin Harcourt Publishing Company.

hmhbooks.com

The number in the mural on page 21 represents those we lost in Hurricane Maria—authorities were still counting at the time this book went to print.

The illustrations in this book were done digitally.
The text type was set in Baskerville.
The display type was set in Goshen.
Book design by Sharismar Rodriguez and Andrea Miller
Hand-lettering by Andrea Miller

Library of Congress Cataloging-in-Publication Data
Names: Ramos, NoNieqa, author. | Escobar, Paola, illustrator.
Title: Beauty woke / by NoNieqa Ramos ; illustrated by Paola Escobar.
Description: Boston : Versify, Houghton Mifflin Harcourt, [2021] |
Audience: Ages 4 to 7. | Audience: Grades K–1. | Summary: Beauty, who is of Taíno Indian, African, and Boricua heritage, was taught to be strong and proud but hatred toward people who look like her bruises her heart until her community opens her eyes to the truth.
Identifiers: LCCN 2019036682 | ISBN 9780358008415 (hardcover)
Subjects: CYAC: Race relations—Fiction. | Prejudices—Fiction. | Racially mixed people—Fiction. | Self-esteem—Fiction. | Family life—Fiction.
Classification: LCC PZ7.1.R3656 Be 2021 | DDC [E]—dc23
LC record available at https://lccn.loc.gov/2019036682

Manufactured in Italy
RILO 10 9 8 7 6 5 4 3 2 1
4500835686